T0197522

Kijo

The Secret Celebrity

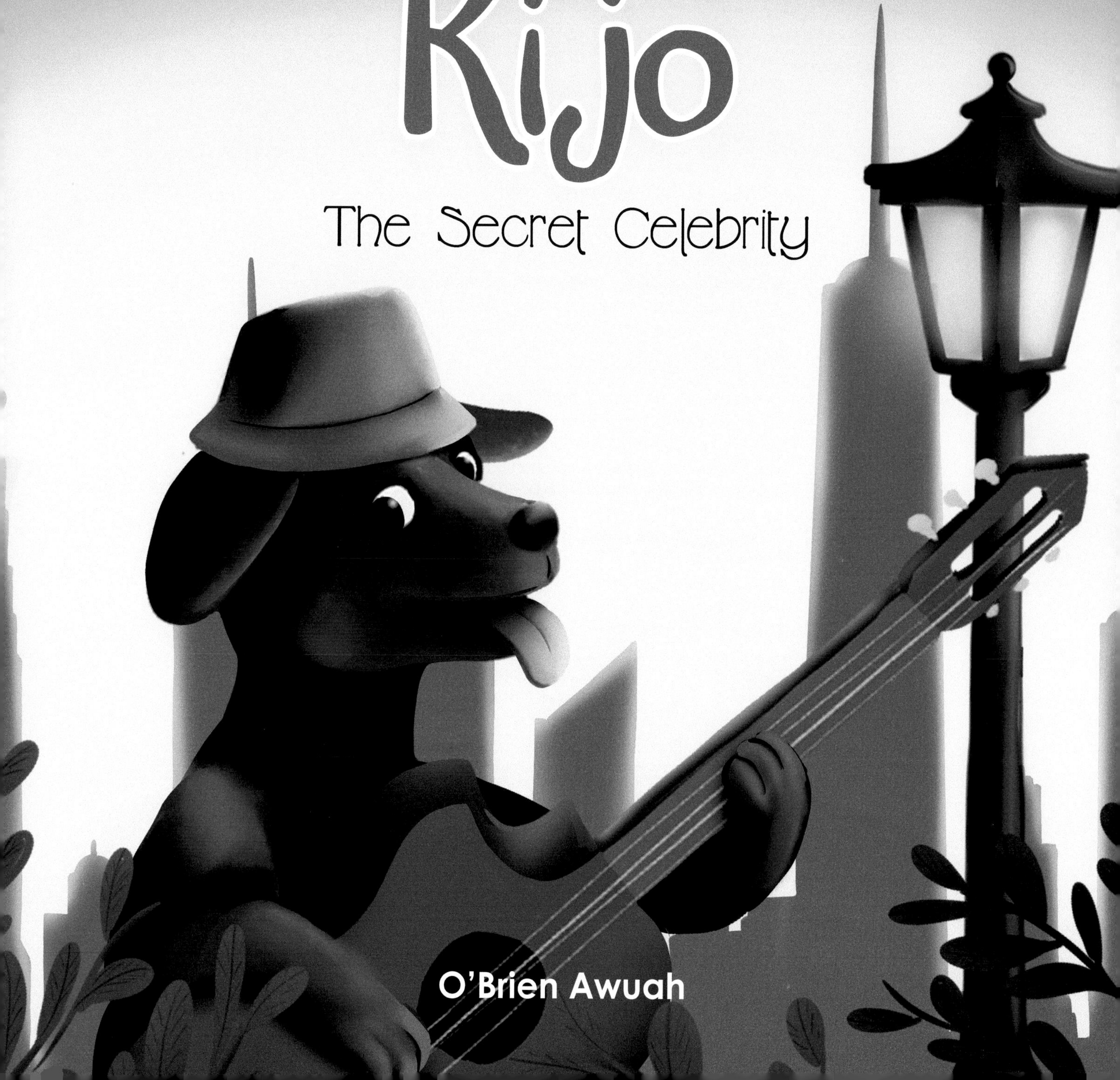

O'Brien Awuah

To order additional copies of this book, contact:
Xlibris
844-714-8691
www.Xlibris.com
Orders@Xlibris.com

ISBN: Softcover   978-1-6641-9718-3
        EBook   978-1-6641-9717-6

Print information available on the last page

Rev. date: 11/10/2021

Kijo

The Secret Celebrity

Kijo

"Hey, kid, that was a good one," Keye, one of the most famous dogs in New York City, commended Kijo as he displayed some excellent dancing skills to the tune of Haddick's guitar. Keye's owner was one of the most affluent businessmen in New York. His residence was right on the upper side of Broadway, so whenever Keye was driven by Columbus Circle, he peeped to watch Kijo and his owner perform at the circle. Zack would steal a glance while driving. He would nod and would hit his steering wheel cautiously in sync with the tune of Haddick's guitar.

Haddick was well-known for his guitar skills in Harlem. He played for a couple of small bands on weekends. He got very busy in the summer when the demand for live music in bars and restaurants was very high. His audience loved his skills, and he was really a fun guy. Kijo would lay right beside him, whirling his hairy tail to and fro to his owner's tunes.

Unfortunately, Haddick's left leg was amputated on his fifty-sixth birthday due to his uncontrolled diabetes. As a result of his disability and long stay in the hospital to treat other complications of diabetes, his band hired a new guitarist. After his discharge, he tried other bands, but he never got hired. Sadly, his landlord evicted him because he could not afford to pay his rent. At last, he became homeless.

The Columbus Circle is one of the busiest places in New York. Thousands of pedestrians admire its beauty. Daily, hundreds of pedestrians stop by for few minutes to either relax or take photos of the beautiful scenes around the Columbus Circle. During the day, you could see well-dressed horses lined up at the edge of Central Park and Columbus Circle, waiting to take tourists to observe the beautiful scenes of Central Park.

Tourists would cheer Kijo as he flipped around and stood on his hind limbs while dancing. Passersby always got caught up with Kijo's dance, and they would throw a few quarters into Haddick's bowl. On a good day, he would make $100. Kijo got disappointed sometimes when the day went bad. He would think his efforts did not yield enough excitement, and that might have fetched them a small amount of money.

Early each morning, while lying beside Haddick in the pedestrian walkway on Central Park Avenue, Kijo would worriedly watch other dogs taken for a walk by either their owners or dog walkers. He always wished he had the same privilege. Sometimes, he would receive a "hello" from some of his friends, and he would respond coldly. Sadly, most of his friends who lived comfortably in apartments disregarded him due to his homelessness. Worse, some of the pets consistently would discourage him when entertaining his fans.

Nakie: Hahaha, look at that kid. What is he doing?

Timmy: Dancing, of course!

Nakie: Whaaaat! too bad"

"Haha haaaaaa!" both giggled at Kijo as their owner drove by Columbus Circle. They consistently discouraged Kijo every time they passed by.

Even though the poor puppy got frustrated sometimes, he never gave up on Haddick. He danced joyfully to entertain his fans. However, the disappointment set in when he lay by his snoring master at night.

One cold morning, Kijo woke up very excited to start the day with his new dancing skills. He had dreamt about his skills the previous night and was very eager to display them to entertain his observers. He thought that would fetch Haddick a lot of money on that fateful day. Kijo woke up an hour earlier and rehearsed his new moves before the game began at the circle.

Haddick usually woke up before New York's rush hour to avoid the loud honking from the city's taxi drivers. Kijo tried waking up his master, but he was unresponsive. Sadly, Haddick had died from complications of diabetes that night. What a pity! Kijo lay beside his master, very depressed. He wished he could speak like humans to tell the pedestrians his master was dead, but he couldn't.

"Hahaha, lalalala! The poor kid is crying. What's wrong, kid?" Timmy asked teasingly as he peed, while his walker stared steadily at the poor homeless man.

"Haddick is dead," Kijo responded as tears ran down his cheeks.

"When is the wake and funeral?" Nakie said jokingly as he signaled Timmy to walk away.

A few minutes later, a pedestrian observed the strange state of Haddick and called 911.

As the emergency services and police approached with loud beeping of their sirens, Kijo got scared and swiftly disappeared from the scene. All his fans were disappointed that day for not watching him and his master, unaware of the death of Haddick. Some thought they might see them the next day. To their dismay, there was a poster of Haddick with a sad heading, "Dead".

Kijo ran as fast as he could without looking back. He managed to cross the Central Park to the East Side, on Sixty-Eighth and Fifth Avenue. He hid quietly behind a pile of garbage at the corner of Sixty-Eighth.

He lay panting, trying to forget about the death of his master, and vowed never to return to the West Side. As he kept sobbing, Leo, one of the smartest dogs who lived at a shelter, had sneaked out as usual to have fun at Central Park. As Leo comfortably raised his left leg in an attempt to pee at the piled garbage, Kijo sneezed very loudly, causing Leo to jump from the walkway into the busy street. As he gazed through the garbage, he saw a poor black puppy shivering. He drew closer and secretly took Kijo to the shelter after listening to his story. The puppy disappeared, and no one, except Leo, knew his whereabouts.

One warm evening, Jet, Quicky, and Moller met at Central Park, New York, during a walk with their owners. The new friends had an exciting time for the first time. Jet's owner, a well-educated sixty-year-old, had Jet as her fiftieth birthday present from her late husband. Mr. and Mrs. Ridge used to walk Jet together at Central Park twice daily, morning and late afternoon. It was their daily routine until Mr. Ridge died a year after his retirement. Since his death, Mrs. Ridge had been suffering from depression, and Jet

was her companion since she was childless. Mrs. Ridge could not walk her pet twice but once every late afternoon. Since Jet now went out once daily and sometimes stayed indoors all day watching his depressed mistress, whenever he got out of his boundaries, he would want to spend much time enjoying the fresh air at Central Park.

Unfortunately, Jet's owner would send him home when all his friends were around and playing together. Jet would walk tearfully behind his mistress and wished Mr. Ridge was around.

Picket: "Hey, J, I will see you tomorrow." That was Jet's new cute friend he met one afternoon. She was one of the prettiest female dogs on Fifth Avenue. Her owner was one of the most famous beauticians in New York City. She went to the park elegantly dressed—her hair well-trimmed with beautiful ribbons on her semi-braided hair. She called Jet J.

Jet would lay quietly at the balcony on the seventh floor, watching other pets play excitedly at the park. Tears would run down his tears as he wished he could play at length with his friends.

One quiet afternoon, Jet had finished eating and was waiting for Mrs. Ridge to take him out. He sat patiently, gazing at his depressed mistress lazily reclining on her couch. Sadly, Jet slept as he waited for hours without any hope of going out. In his sleep, he dreamt of a beautiful city beneath Central Park. He saw all his friends playing endlessly. He had ample time with Picket, his new friend. The city was very busy with different pets. They went about their businesses, drove their own cars, had their own leaders, and were independent of their owners.

Unfortunately, a loud honking from a yellow cab on Fifth Avenue suddenly woke him up. Hastily, he ran to his balcony and smiled while gazing at Central Park. He wished his dream became a reality.

The next day, Jet was fortunate to go to the park with his mistress. He was so anxious to disclose his dream to his friends at the park. He pulled Mrs. Ridge so hard that she almost fell. Surprisingly, Jet's friends were not available when he got there. He saw new pets arounds but had no interest in playing with them. As he was about to be pulled out, he saw Picket walking cautiously with Ms. Rowette. Picket's hair was well-groomed, her ribbons matching her fine dress.

In fact, she attracted every pedestrian that set eyes on her. As Jet saw her, he ran to meet her.

Picket: Hey, J, I didn't see you yesterday. I felt lonely even though other friends were here.

Jet: I am so sorry. My mistress could not bring me to play. I had an interesting dream, and I want to quickly share it with you before I leave.

Picket: Tell me, dear.

After narrating the dream to Picket, she exclaimed and jumped excitedly.

Picket: Wooooooooow, what an interesting dream! Since you are leaving, I will take my time to discuss it with Mollar and Quicky. I hope they will be glad to hear this.

Jet: I will really appreciate it, bye.

Both pets hugged, and Jet left with his mistress.

Before long Mollar and Quicky entered the park from the West side.

Picket: Hey, guys, I am here.

Picket barked to draw the attention of her friends.

Mollar: There she comes, our charming friend.

Quicky: Always charming. I wish eeem—

Mollar: Stop right there, I can read your mind.

Quicky: Seriously?

Both dogs walked to meet Picket.

Quicky: Hey, what's up?

Picket: Jet had a dream, and I think you will love to hear it.

Mollar stepped forward. "Tell us."

Picket patiently narrated the dream to her friends.

Mollar: Wo, wo, woo, very interesting. This sounds like a prophecy and must come true.

Picket: How?

Mollar: We can build a very beautiful city beneath this park. It will be our paradise, no owners, and we can play without any distraction from our owners. Also, it can be the first pet city in the world. We will have our own leaders, security personnel, cars, schools, hospitals, entertainment centers, and—

Quicky: Recreational parks.

Mollar: Excellent.

As the meeting was progressing, Picket's mistress was on her cell phone, busily transacting a $50,000 deal with a renowned fashion industry in New York. There was an upcoming fashion week at the fashion district in New York, and the organizers needed a professional beautician to provide makeup and hairstyle services to their models.

Ms. Rowette: Yes, yes, yes, thank you God.

She jumped excited after winning the deal.

Ms. Rowette: Pickeeeeeet, it is time to go, hurry up, cutie.

Quicky: I think we have to work as soon as possible to build our dream city.

Picket: What is the plan?

Picket walked toward her mistress while looking at her friends.

Mollar: Don't worry, I will write letters to invite all pets in New York for an emergency meeting. I hope they will love this idea.

Picket: Great idea, see you later, guys.

Among the four dogs, Mollar was the most brilliant. He was a fast learner. His owners were British Americans, and both were professors of literature in New York. He could read and write very well. His friends would make fun of his British accent when playing.

A week later, he had written more than fifteen thousand letters to be distributed to pets in New York. In fact, rats played a major role in the distribution. They sent out ten thousand letters via the train to pets in the five boroughs of New York City, and doves distributed the rest. More than ten thousand pets responded positively to build the proposed city beneath Central Park. All the pets convened at the Metropolitan Museum of Arts on Fifth Avenue at midnight. They managed to find a secret entrance to the museum.

Kit, the oldest cat on Fifth Avenue came very late. She walked slowly, squeezed herself among the dogs from the back, and sat right in front of Mollar. Even though the rats were not pets, they were invited because of the major role they would play in the construction of the city. They would help with all the tunnels. They sat far from the cats to avoid confrontations between them.

Before the meeting started, Mollar had consulted Peeka. He was one of the finest architects in New York. His master was one of the most experienced architects in New York. He designed the high-rise buildings and hotels in New York. Peeka developed most of his skills from his owner. Pets experienced at road construction, IT experts, media experts, plumbers, and security experts came together and designed a beautiful city. After an excellent presentation, all the pets loved the plan and were all onboard, except Kit.

Kit cleared her throat and spoke out, "I love my bed. I am not going to wake up at night and walk in my sleep to the so-called Secret City. In fact, I don't think any cat will be part of this idea because we love to sleep. I am afraid myself and all other cats will sleep when we meet in the city. Therefore, I totally disagree with this idea."

Suddenly, the whole museum was filled with murmurs.

Unfortunately, most cats were in favor of the idea after a vote. Peeka left the meeting with great disappointment. He left hurriedly before everyone else.

There was a massive cheer up after the meeting. All the pets were so happy and were eager to build the city in a short time frame. A year later, the Secret City was built. All the pets put together great skills and constructed a beautiful city beneath Central Park.

The opening ceremony was very beautiful. Each pet was dressed in a grand style. It was really an exciting day to witness. Fortunately, the opening of the first pet city coincided with a United Nations Summit in New York. That was the first time the White House dog was traveling with the president. A secret letter had already been given to the White House dog, so he decided to take that opportunity to open the Secret City. Every pet in New York was very happy and eager to meet the president's pet. All security measures were in place to escort the special guest from his hotel to Central Park. In fact, the rats did a great job by creating a tunnel to transport the White House pet to the city.

Mollar: The day has finally come when pets are independent of their owners, socialize without hindrances, and enjoy the serenity of our own city.

All the pets applauded with a loud cheer as a soft song played in the background. Fireworks were heard in the background, and the sky was beaming with bright lights.

Keith: Now, Mr. president, ladies and gentlemen, this is one of the most important moments in today's gathering. We are all witnessing this fateful day because of the hard work of some great thinkers among us. Truly, these people have contributed immensely to the building of our beautiful secret city. We cannot leave here without honoring them. But before this ceremony, there is a talented young artist among us. Some of you may have seen him, or it may be the first time seeing him. Among the several pet musicians and dancers, he is number one. Shall we please welcome on stage Kiii-jooo as he performs the main song for this memorable occasion.

Leo: Woo, woooo, that's my boy.

Timmy and Nakie were right at the front row wondering if that was the puppy they knew on Central Park Avenue. They could not believe their eyes when Kijo was climbing the stage, dressed in a fine leather jacket with a well-designed hat, eager to shake his audience.

Timmy: Impossible, impossible! I thought he was dead.

Nakie: I don't think I can watch this, I have to pee.

Hurriedly, Nakie left the crowd in shame.

In fact, that was Kijo's best performance ever. Leo really did a great job training him at the shelter. Kijo's performance moved the White House pet, and he was given a special award. Life for Kijo and Leo turned successful in the Secret City. Since then, Kijo became a famous artiste in the Secret City. He remained at the shelter until he was adopted by Dr. Vicki Flaris, Ph.D., a very kind professor of chemistry in New York.

The End

Reflection

Answer these questions after reading the book:

1. How would you describe the character of Timmy and Nakie?

2. How would you react if friends like Timmy and Nakie consistently discourage you every time you make an attempt in life?

3. What has inspired you about Mollar and his friends after they heard Jet's dream?

4. What did you learn about Leo?

5. Overall, how would you relate Kijo's efforts to your personal life?